THE BOOK
THAT DID NOT
WANT TO
BE READ

DAVID ✦ SUNDIN

*Psst... reading a book that doesn't
want to be read can be very hard.
Almost impossible. Maybe you should
read a different book instead?*

Translated by B. J. Woodstein

SIMON & SCHUSTER BOOKS FOR YOUNG READERS
New York London Toronto Sydney New Delhi

nce upon a time, there was a child who couldn't fall asleep.

So the child asked a grown-up, "Can you please read me a book?"

 AND THE GROWN-UP SAID, » Of course I can! «

❖ *The grown-up shouldn't have done that.* ❖
Because the child had found a very special book.
A BOOK THAT DID *NOT* WANT TO BE READ
and it did all it could so that it wouldn't be.

And the story about that book starts now!

Okay...

Hold on!

Here we goo

It started with the book
being transformed into
a steering wheel.
The grown-up had
to steer with it.

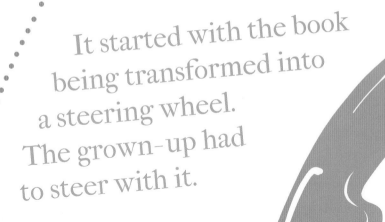

VRRROOM

VRRRRRO

The grown-up
steered to the right.
VROOM VROOM.
And to the leeeeft.
VROOM VROOM.

"BEEP BEEP!" said the grown-up, pressing the steering wheel.

VROOM VROOM.

OOOOOOM!

Then they arrived.

BUT THEN...

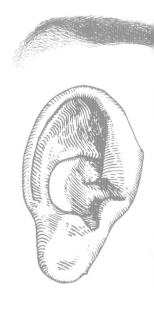

... new words appeared in the book.
Words no one had ever heard beflore.

It suddenly got very blard to fread the book.
There was a baddle that kralled poysh.
Poysh? Yes, poysh.

The grown-up had never before had
to read a book that was so awkword!

The grown-up checked to see if the child had fallen asleep. Nope. Not yet. Must keep reading then.

When the dog's farty was pinished, everyone wanted to spling to the marmelady. They all got marmelady in their flurb and flod into a lorfer. Plimkom fadde trattels nabui. Yabey, yabey, dabb. Bollibolli gat got nabb.

THE GROWN-UP SIGHED LOUDLY.

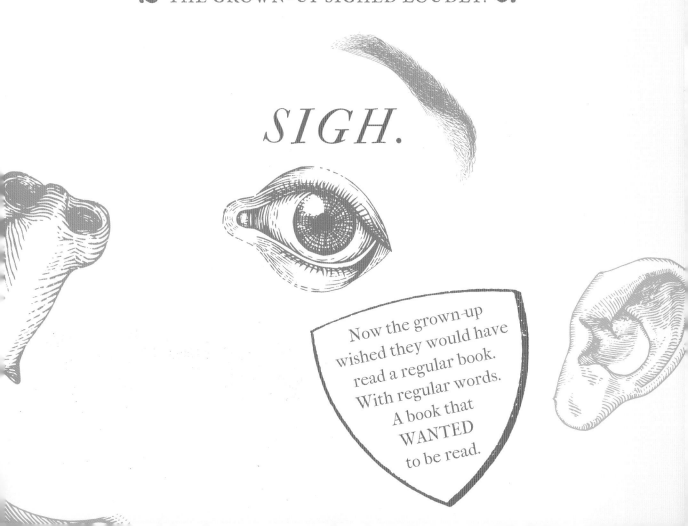

SIGH.

Now the grown-up wished they would have read a regular book. With regular words. A book that WANTED to be read.

Then the book grew
WINGS!

And it started flap-flap-
flapping around like a bird.

The grown-up had to hold on tight to
the book so it wouldn't fly out of the window.

Flap flap!

HEEELP!!!!

The grown-up had to lie on the book and count to 10.

Then the grown-up checked to see if the book was behaving any better.

It wasn't.
Because now the text
got smaller and smaller

and smaller.

You could hardly read
what it said in the book.

You had to look very closely.

You don't look that smart when
you're looking at a book so closely.

Wonder what it says here?

But then

the text got

bigger again!

Bigger!

And bigger!

And bigge

And b

igger!

BEHAVE, BOOK.

Suddenly, there was a picture of a rabbit that did not have anything to do with anything.

"Hi there," the grown-up said to the rabbit.

Haha, the grown-up didn't understand
that it wasn't a real rabbit.
It was just a picture.

"Oh, you cutie-patootie," said the grown-up,
petting the picture of the rabbit.

Then the grown-up whispered to the child
what the name of the rabbit was,
so quietly that no one could hear it.

Then it said that it was

THE END

of the book and you
absolutely weren't allowed
to turn the page.

But the grown-up and the child turned the page anyway...

The book started to close.

Oh, no! The book is closing! Stop it!

The grown-up
had to really
grip it hard so the
book wouldn't close.

Come on!

Fiiight it!

Then the grown-up started hearing music that no one else could hear, and instead of reading, the grown-up had to sing.

"Ooohhh,

Why

how I love to reeeaaad this book. . . .

This is the best book I have ever reeaad.

won't the child sleeeeep?

Is it because I'm siiiingiiiing?

Oh bop a lula."

"How nicely I sing," the grown-up said.
The child just shook their head.

Wait a minute…
The book is starting to feel…
a little *warm*?

Oh, no!

THE BOOK
IS ON FIRE!

Ouch!

It burns if
you touch *here*!

Ouch!

Or if you touch it *here*!

"We have to bloooow!
Help me blow!"
said the grown-up.

Whooooosh!

PHEW!
WELL DONE.

Now maybe we'll have
some peace and quiet,
thought the grown-up.
Maybe the book will be more
like a regular book now.
A book that wants to be read.

BUT NO...

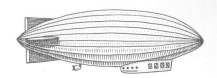

Because now words were
DISAPPEARING out of the book.
So the grown-up just had to make up words
wherever they were missing. Have fun.

Once upon a time, there was an outstanding

..........who had to go to .... On the way there,

.... and then .... a green banjo ....

that .... Then .... tried to

.... and it went .... well.

But wait! Didn't it smell a little ...... here?

It wasn't .... that had ....

Then .... and .... lived

happily for ....

"Do we have to go on?" asked the grown-up.
"Yes, we do," said the child.

Help!

A A A A A A A A A...

All the As had suddenly
changed into Os.

"Thot wos not funny,"
soid the grown-up.
"Whot if on olligotor comes
and I must scream,

'WOTCH OUT FOR THE OLLIGOTOR!'

Moybe no one could heor me
ond they would be eoten
by the olligotor!

Bod news. Very bod. And sod.

Reolly sod."

But finally.

(After a picture of a hat)

When the grown-up had struggled
and struggled and struggled and
made things up and sung and fought
and struggled and blown and read
and steered and struggled and
struggled and struggled,

then the child said,
"I want to sleep now.
Good night."

And so the grown-up said,
"Good night, my darling."

And then it was

THE END.

. . . or was it?

It was <u>definitely</u> *not* the end!

Got you!

Haha!

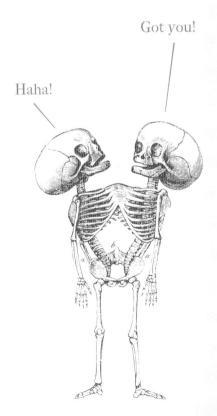

the book

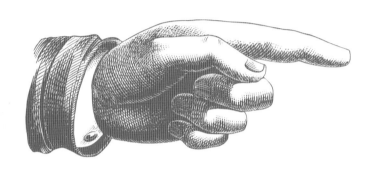

Suddenly

so it

became

to run

started

words in
around

difficult

to read.

The text spun all the way around. "Another spin!" said the child.

grown-up had to turn the book around to read it. 🖐

It was a bit tricky when the book first ended up this way.

And then this way. Now the book was upside-down 🖐

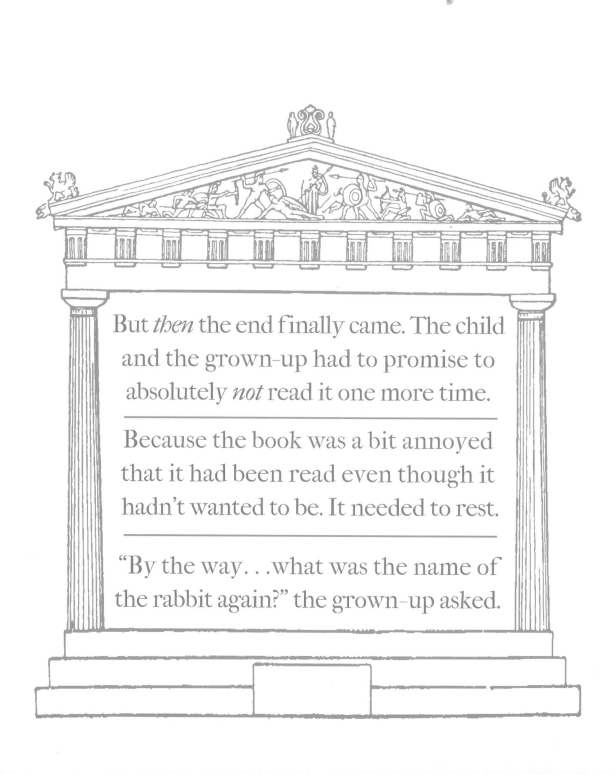

But *then* the end finally came. The child and the grown-up had to promise to absolutely *not* read it one more time.

Because the book was a bit annoyed that it had been read even though it hadn't wanted to be. It needed to rest.

"By the way. . .what was the name of the rabbit again?" the grown-up asked.

THEN THE GROWN-UP
SAID TO THE CHILD:
"Don't forget that you're the best.
YOU CAN BE WHATEVER
YOU WANT TO BE.
I love you.
Hugs and kisses.
SWEET DREAMS."

SIMON & SCHUSTER BOOKS FOR YOUNG READERS
An imprint of Simon & Schuster Children's Publishing Division • 1230 Avenue of
the Americas, New York, New York 10020 • © 2020 by David Sundin • English
language translation © 2022 by Simon & Schuster, Inc. • Originally published
in Sweden in 2020 by Bonnier Carlsen as *Boken som inte ville bli läst* •
Published by agreement with Salomonsson Agency. • First US Edition 2022
• Jacket design by Lucy Ruth Cummins © 2022 by Simon & Schuster, Inc.
SIMON & SCHUSTER BOOKS FOR YOUNG READERS and related
marks are trademarks of Simon & Schuster, Inc. • For information about special
discounts for bulk purchases, please contact Simon & Schuster Special Sales at
1-866-506-1949 or business@simonandschuster.com. • The Simon & Schuster
Speakers Bureau can bring authors to your live event. For more information or
to book an event, contact the Simon & Schuster Speakers Bureau at 1-866-248-
3049 or visit our website at www.simonspeakers.com. • The text for this book was
set in IM FELL French Canon PRO. • The illustrations for this book were rendered
digitally. • Manufactured in China • 1121 SCP • 2 4 6 8 10 9 7 5 3 1 •
CIP data for this book is available from the Library of Congress. •
ISBN 978-1-6659-1081-1 • ISBN 978-1-6659-1082-8 (ebook)